GW00393867

Copyright © 2020 by Lina Mirrow

All rights reserved.

No part of this book may be reproduced, distributed, or transmitted in any form or by any means, including photocopying, recording, or other electronic or mechanical methods, without the prior written permission of the publisher, except in the case of brief quotations embodied in critical reviews and certain other noncommercial uses permitted by copyright law. For permission requests, write to the publisher, addressed "Attention: Permissions Coordinator," at the address below.

SWEET BATTLE

Aunt Broccoli vs. Sir Caramel

Author: Lina Mirrow
Illustrator: Viktoria Soltis-Doan
Idea:Lina Mirrow

Every morning
I started my day the same way.

I got up from my warm, cosy bed...

I got dressed into my green T-shirt with stars and some bright, orange trousers ...

I brushed my curly blonde hair...

And I headed straight to Aunt Broccoli's Café.

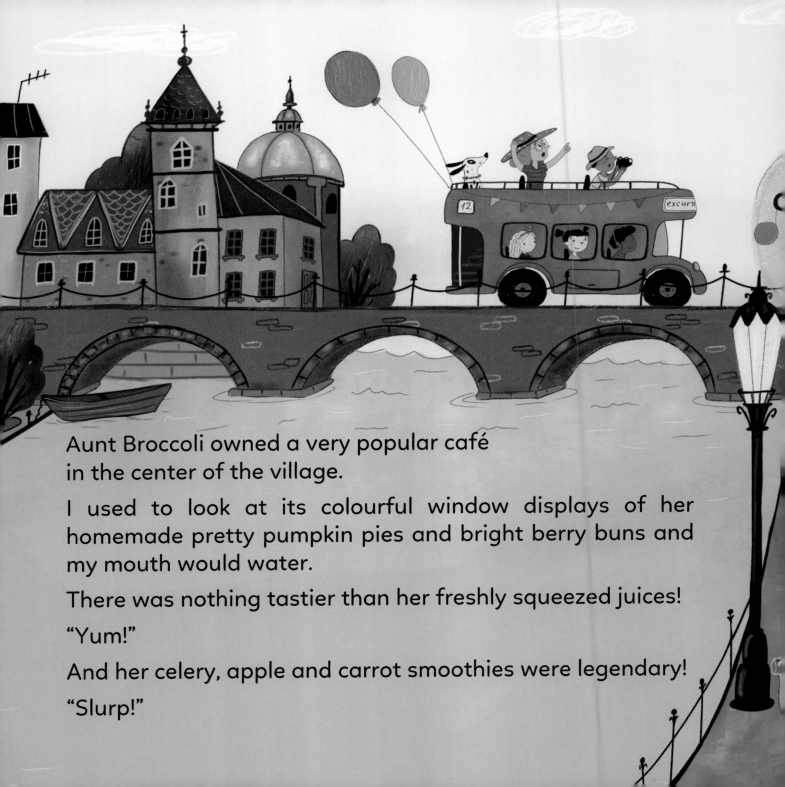

Aunt Broccoli owned a very popular café in the center of the village.

I used to look at its colourful window displays of her homemade pretty pumpkin pies and bright berry buns and my mouth would water.

There was nothing tastier than her freshly squeezed juices!

"Yum!"

And her celery, apple and carrot smoothies were legendary!

"Slurp!"

So, on our way to school, my friends and I always stopped by her café for a delicious glass of juice, some oatmeal and a crunchy almond cookie.

EVERYTHING smelled sooo DEEEEE...LICIOUS here!!

If only I could try the WHOLE menu and bring it to school.

I would share it with ALL my friends...

then EVERYONE would be happy and healthy.

That was, until the ARRIVAL of cunning Sir Caramel

who SUDDENLY appeared in a whirlwind of sweets.

"Crash... Bang... Wallop!"

He entered our village on his high-speed motorcycle, WHIZZING and WHOOSHING... throwing around wrappers of sweets which he had LOTS OF under his cloak!

I could see him grinning under his thick moustache as he watched my friends chomping on chocolate and licking lollipops.

The evil Sir Caramel knew how to trick children into eating his sweets!!!

Sir Caramel drove his twinkly Sweet Carousel around, while selling candy and ice-cream to all the children.

Soon there was chaos in the village!

'EEEEEK!'

All my friends started stuffing their faces with all different kinds of SWEET THINGS!

They started by eating candy floss and cupcakes for BREAKFAST.

LUNCH was made up of chocolate doughnuts and cookies.

At DINNER time they had macaroons and marshmallows!

The more sugar they ate, the more they wanted.

When the day was over and the children were sleeping SWEETLY in their beds... 'ZZZZzzzzz',

Sir Caramel was busy plotting his next potions in his TOP SECRET LAB.

ALL you could hear was BURBLING and GURGLING.

You see... sneaky Sir Caramel had put a secret potion into the soda to make the children forget about ANY healthy food, so they would buy more of his sweets. How crafty of him?!

The poor children became weaker and weaker by the day.

They no longer wanted to run or jump.

They weren't interested in learning new things and soon, they even stopped coming to school!

They sat around all day, moaning and groaning.

'Ahhh!'

Their tummies hurt, and so did their teeth.

'Ohhh!'

Life was no longer fun for my friends, and soon the village streets became empty. There was no longer the echo of children's laughter or the sound of their feet running up and down the park.

Nobody went to the café.

Nobody cared for a healthy breakfast anymore.

I was very worried. So, I ran to Aunt Broccoli's house and banged on her door.

Aunt Broccoli hurried to let me in. I could see it in her face that she was worried too.

"We have to come up with a plan to save my friends!" I said.

Aunt Broccoli thought about it.

"I might have exactly what we need!" she said, searching for her big recipe book.

"But we'll need help, and I know just who to call."

Soon, her friends – The Vitamins– came to the rescue.

We stayed up all night making a magical healthy concoction of fruit and vegetables.

It looked wonderful!

I gave it a little try. It tasted wonderful too.

"Mmmmmmm!"

One by one, my friends tried Aunt Broccoli's Super Smoothies.

At last, almost by magic, they became strong and healthy once again.

They were so happy that they started to dance, jump and yell 'Woohoo!'

The sneaky Sir Caramel was banished from the village by Aunt Broccoli and her friends, as the children stopped eating his sugary food.

He quickly wrapped up his nasty treats and ran away on his carousel.

No one knows where he went. But if you ever see him, STAY AWAY!

AUNT BROCCOLI'S SECRETS

Aunt Broccoli always tells me, "Eat healthy food and you will grow strong and smart."

"But what is healthy food?" I ask.

She takes me to her garden, spreads her arms and says, "All of this!"

I look at her magnificent bushes of fragrant sweet strawberries and ripe raspberries.

Did I mention the huge fruit trees with rosy apples and dark plums?!

If you look over to the vegetable patch, you will find my favourite juicy tomatoes and the little cucumbers.

We pick some of them.

"Now, let's go make some healthy meals," she says,

"It's going to be a busy day at the café tomorrow."